Germy Johnson's
SECRET PLAN

Alison Lohans

Cover by
Janet Wilson

Scholastic Canada Ltd.

Canadian Cataloguing in Publication Data

Lohans, Alison, 1949-
    Germy Johnson's secret plan

(Shooting star)
ISBN 0-590-71671-9

I. Wilson, Janet, 1952- . II. Title.
III. Series.

PS8573.035G4 1992   jC813'.54   C91-095297-3
PZ7.L65Ge 1992

6 5 4 3 2 1   Printed in Canada   2 3 4 5 6/9
                Manufactured by Webcom Limited

Contents

For John and Christopher
with love
and for Jill

Chapter 1

Bad News

"Jeremy Johnson!"

J.J. jumped.

Mrs. Foley was looking right at him. "For the second time, Jeremy, are you feeling all right?"

J.J. stared down at his desk. He hated being called Jeremy. "I'm OK," he said. Actually, he wasn't OK. His stomach felt awful. But Mrs. Foley was reading a good book, and he didn't want to miss anything. It was called *One Chance to Win*, and it was about a boy who got a job working in a kennel.

J.J. wanted a dog so much. He wiggled his fingers, and his hand could almost feel a dog's silky head. In fact, he could almost *see* the dog, with brown smiley eyes and a wagging tail. It would be cool to run around the back yard with his dog. But Mom and Dad said that dogs were too much trouble.

Mrs. Foley went back to the story. The kennel was on fire! The owners were away, and Wink had to save the dogs!

J.J. felt sicker and sicker. All of a sudden he threw up all over his desk.

The class was silent. J.J. could feel his neck getting hot, but he was almost too sick to care.

Mrs. Foley closed the book. "Why don't you go to the nurse's office, Jeremy."

Kyle leaned toward J.J. *"Germy Johnson!"* he whispered. Somebody giggled. J.J.'s ears got hot too.

"Not feeling so good, J.J.?" asked Mrs. Moosomin, the nurse.

"I'm sick," he moaned, and lay down on the cot. Mrs. Moosomin gave him a thermometer.

"Oh boy," said Mrs. Moosomin when she read the thermometer. "You have a fever. I'll phone your mom and ask her to come get you."

J.J. went outside to wait.

All the trees were yellow. Thanksgiving was coming in a few days. But J.J. didn't care. All he knew was that he felt awful. He lay down on the grass and looked at the sky.

Something soft brushed against his cheek.

"Yeow!" J.J. sat up in a hurry.

"Meow." A dirty kitten climbed into his lap. It was white all over except for yellow ears and a yellow striped tail.

J.J. felt silly. He looked around sheepishly. "What do you think you're doing?" he said to the cat. "Sneaking around scaring people."

The kitten stuck its pink nose into J.J.'s face and started purring like a little motor. It had black grease on its tail, and one foot looked sore.

A car honked. Mom was waiting, with Jessica in her baby seat in the back. "I've got to go," J.J. told the kitten.

The kitten followed him to the car. When he

sat down in the front seat, the kitten did a neat little jump and landed in his lap.

"You poor boy," Mom said. "You look pale."

"Look, Mom," said J.J. He petted the kitten.

Mom smiled. "Better put it out, J.J. We need to go."

Very carefully J.J. set the kitten on the sidewalk. Before he had a chance to shut the door, the kitten jumped back in. It climbed up the back of the seat and looked over.

"Gee!" Jessica laughed. "Gee" was her word for kitty.

"I'll put him out," Mom said. She scooped up the kitten and got out.

"Meoooooowwwww," said the kitten. J.J. could hear it scratching against the car door. *"Meooooooooowwwwww."* It sounded like it was crying.

For some reason J.J. didn't feel quite so sick anymore. "He's crying, Mom," he said. "Can't we take him home? He's all dirty and his foot is hurt. I bet he doesn't have a home."

His mother started the car.

He couldn't just leave the kitten at school, J.J. knew. Shaun Higgins might throw rocks at it. And what if it rained? Or snowed? J.J. opened the door, just a little.

The kitten scrambled back into his lap.

"J.J. . . ." Mom warned. But she looked at the kitten and sighed. "It could be a stray. Honestly, some people are cruel — dumping animals off to fend for themselves."

"You mean we can keep him?" J.J. felt even better.

"We'll see," said Mom. "Right now I have other things to think about."

The minute J.J. walked into his room he found out what she meant. *Mom! Where's all my stuff?*

His toys were gone. His shelves were gone. So were most of his clothes.

"That's what I needed to tell you," Mom called. "Aunt Pru is coming for a long visit. I hate to do this, J.J., but you'll have to share with Jessica while Aunt Pru is here."

Suddenly J.J. felt sicker than ever. He flopped

down on the bed and played dead. But a purring, furry little body kept rubbing against his face, pushing its cold wet nose and tickly whiskers into his ear. It made him giggle.

Aunt Pru was old. She had orange hair. She smelled like medicine. Her false teeth clicked when she talked, and sometimes she took them out to surprise people. When he was little he had been scared of Aunt Pru's teeth. Even now they made him feel all squirmy inside.

And now she was going to live in his *bedroom . . .*

Chapter 2

A Wild Bath

J.J. was sick for two days. He tried to stay sick longer, hoping maybe Aunt Pru wouldn't come. But on the third day Mom took his temperature, nodded and sent him back to school. When he got home his bed had clean sheets and a new pillow. Mom said from now on he had to sleep on the cot in Jessica's room.

"Don't worry, J.J." Mom patted his shoulder. "Everything will work out."

J.J. wasn't so sure.

At least there was *some* good news. Mom and Dad had decided the kitten could stay, since nobody had answered their Lost-and-Found ad in the paper. Mom took the kitten to the vet for shots and bought cat food. J.J. could hardly believe his luck. A cat! It wasn't a dog, but it was definitely a start.

"Well, J.J.," said Dad that evening. "What are you going to call your cat?"

J.J. had been thinking about names, but so far nothing seemed right. "Um, Comet? Snowball?"

"Gee!" cried Jessica. She was just learning to walk. She tried to run to the kitten, but she sat down by mistake.

The kitten jumped onto Dad's chair and batted at the newspaper. "I know a name," said Dad. "Brat Cat."

"Dad!" J.J. protested.

Dad grinned. "That can be his nickname, when he gets in trouble." He looked at his watch. "Well, it's almost time to go pick up Aunt Pru."

J.J. had been trying not to think about Aunt Pru. Now she was on her way, on the bus. Once she and Dad got back from the bus station, they'd all have cookies and ice cream. Then it would be bedtime. On the cot. In Jessica's room. Why couldn't Aunt Pru share with Jessica instead?

Without warning, the kitten tackled his foot. Tiny sharp claws and teeth dug through his sock. "Yeow!" cried J.J. Dogs never did that. Why couldn't a puppy have found him instead? But then the kitten jumped up and looked at him with its big blue eyes. It started to purr.

J.J. stroked the cat's soft furry head. It rubbed against him and settled into a nice warm lump in his lap, so he sat there petting it and reading *One Chance to Win*. Mrs. Foley had let him bring the book home since he'd missed the ending.

Soon it was bath time. Mom wouldn't let him take books into the bathroom, so J.J. took the kitten instead.

He turned on the water hard so it sounded like a herd of dinosaurs was running through the bathtub. The kitten jumped up on the sink to watch.

J.J. pretended his legs were sea monsters. He shook the wash cloth to shoot wet bullets at them. The kitten jumped onto the edge of the tub to watch.

"Hi, Comet," he said. "Hi, Snowball." But the names didn't seem to fit. He held the wash cloth up high so water trickled down in a silver streak.

The kitten batted at the water. Then it backed up and licked its paw. The water kept coming. The kitten reached out . . . farther . . . and slid into the tub with a splash.

For an instant the water churned as if there were a real sea monster in there. Then the kitten shot out, spraying water everywhere. J.J. started to laugh. The kitten raced around the edge of the tub. When it got to the faucets it ran out of space. *Splash!* It plunged in again, then scrambled up J.J.'s arm.

"Yeow!" cried J.J.

The kitten leaped to the bath mat and zoomed around like a mad wasp. *Thump!* It jumped against the door, but the door was closed. *Crash!*

It raced across the counter, knocking the toothbrushes down.

"J.J.!" called Mom. "What on earth are you doing in there?"

"Taking my bath." He tried hard not to laugh. *Zap!* The kitten scrambled up a towel and clung there. It didn't look much like a kitten any more. It looked like a wet rat with a long stringy tail. J.J.'s stomach hurt from laughing so hard. *Thunk.* The towel fell down. The kitten scampered to hide behind the toilet. "Meoowwww," it said in a tiny voice.

"J.J.?" Mom was coming! "Time's up."

Quickly J.J. pulled out the plug. "I'm done," he yelled.

Then he heard the front door open. He heard Dad's voice, and Aunt Pru's old sour pickles voice. Mom went back downstairs. "Saved!" said J.J. He dried himself and put on his pajamas. Then he peeked at the kitten and started laughing all over again. He opened the door.

The kitten zoomed out of the bathroom and

streaked downstairs in a soggy white blur. J.J. raced after it. There was a wet trail all the way down the steps. He got to the bottom just in time to see the kitten dash between Aunt Pru's legs.

"Oh!" shrieked Aunt Pru. She fell against Dad. Dad almost tripped over one of Aunt Pru's big suitcases. He caught Aunt Pru just in time.

J.J. tried not to laugh.

"What was that?" Aunt Pru gasped.

Dad was grinning. "That's our newest family member — J.J.'s cat."

Aunt Pru turned to J.J. "Hello, Jeremy," she said, and gave him a kiss. As usual, she smelled like medicine. "My, you've grown." She looked around the room. "Now where's that cat? Did you give him a bath too?"

"He fell in," J.J. explained. He couldn't help laughing all over again, remembering.

"So *that's* what all the crashing was about," said Mom. The corners of her mouth wiggled, but she was holding Jessica and Jessica was reaching for Aunt Pru's nose. Mom moved Jessica just in time.

Aunt Pru smiled at Jessica with her big white false teeth. J.J. wondered if she would take them out to surprise the baby.

She didn't.

Soon Dad had the ice cream and cookies out and they all sat down.

Too soon, it was bedtime.

J.J. had trouble falling asleep. The cot was hard and narrow, and Jessica kept kicking the bars in her crib. Finally she stopped. But still J.J. couldn't sleep. He wished Aunt Pru would go away. It wasn't fair for her to take his room.

After a long time a soft purring lump landed on the cot and snuggled against J.J.'s cheek. At last he fell asleep.

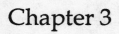

Chapter 3

A Different
Kind Of Bath

"She's *old*," J.J. complained to his friend Derek the next morning at recess. "She smells like medicine. And she takes her false teeth out to surprise people."

"False teeth?" said Derek. "Cool! Can I come see them?"

J.J. shook his head. "Mom said nobody can come over till she's settled in."

"Rats."

J.J. didn't see how anybody could be interested in Aunt Pru's gross false teeth. He kicked a rock. It splashed through a puddle left from last night's rain and hit a bike in the rack.

"Hey, meatface," said a nasty voice. "Touch my bike and you're smeared."

Wouldn't you know it — the bike belonged to Shaun Higgins. "I didn't hurt your old bike," J.J. said, wishing his heart wouldn't jump like a scared rabbit whenever Shaun came around.

"Fine. Then your face won't hurt either when I pound it." Shaun stood there like a mound of mad blubber.

"Better not," warned Derek. "J.J.'s got a pit bull."

J.J. gulped in a deep breath. "Yeah, Shaun," he agreed. "I'll teach him to go for your scent."

Shaun looked at them for a minute as if he wasn't sure. "I bet you're lying," he said. "You'll be in trouble, T-R-U-B-B-E-L, *trouble*." And he walked away as if he owned the whole playground.

"Holy cow!" said Derek. "He *believed* us!"

J.J. was amazed. Suddenly he remembered that he hadn't told Derek about the kitten in the tub. By the time he finished, they were both out of breath from laughing. "The only problem is," J.J. gasped, "I don't know what to call it."

"I know!" Derek punched him in the arm. "Call it Pruneface. Get it? Pruuuuneface, for your Auntie Pru."

"Oh, get out of here," said J.J.

Everyone wanted to help name the kitten. Tanya suggested Orphan. Stephanie said he should call it Lucky, since it found a good home. Trent liked Super Megacat. By the time school was out J.J. was sick of names.

He sloshed through puddles on his way home. He wasn't in much of a hurry. Thanksgiving weekend started tomorrow. Derek was going to Calgary to visit his grandma, so there'd be nobody to play with. Well, Tanya might want to do something. But usually she was too bossy.

A bicycle skimmed past and veered through a puddle. *Slosh!* Water sprayed all over J.J.

"Pit bull!" Shaun yelled, and laughed his crazy laugh.

"Thanks a lot!" J.J. yelled back. But Shaun was already gone. "You old blubber brain," he muttered, wiping the water off his face.

J.J. went down to the river to throw some rocks. Too late, he remembered the mud. It was like clay. With every step he took, more mud stuck to his runners. Soon his feet were as big as footballs.

Gross! Mom wouldn't like that. His runners were still pretty new. He leaned against a tree and tried to scrape the mud off with a stick, but it didn't work. The stick broke and mud smeared all over his hands. He tried scraping his feet against the tree. Some of the mud came off, but somehow it got smeared on his jeans too.

"Oh barf!"

J.J. kicked. A clump of mud the size of a hockey puck flew off and slid down the river bank. He kicked harder. His left shoe came off and sailed toward the river.

He dived for it and grabbed it just in time. When he got up, he heard a strange slurpy sound. He felt heavy and wet all over.

J.J. looked down. His jeans were brown. His blue and yellow windbreaker was brown. His feet were brown and his hands were brown. He was covered with mud from head to foot.

"Oh no!" he moaned. Now he was really in trouble. Mom would be mad. She'd probably throw him in the washing machine along with his clothes.

J.J. sat there on the river bank, thinking.

If he washed himself off in the river, he'd get muddy all over again climbing up the river bank. Besides, it was cold. He could go to the park and roll around on the grass like a dog, but most of the mud would probably stay on. He couldn't go through sprinklers on the way home. Nobody watered their lawns in October.

J.J. sighed. The only thing to do was go home. He got up and trudged down the street, wishing he was invisible.

Mr. Lim's dog gave him a funny look and backed off.

"*Grrr!*" J.J. growled. The dog ran away.

Tanya's little sister Amy was walking along swinging her purse at all the bushes. When she saw J.J., she backed off too.

"*Grrr!*" J.J. said. He even scared Mrs. Tillis' cat. Being muddy all over was actually kind of fun. "I'm the creature from the Black Lagoon," he said.

And then he sighed with relief. Mom's car was gone. She must be shopping. He could hide his muddy clothes under the bed. He reached for his key and fumbled with the doorknob. But the house was unlocked.

"Jeremy?" called Aunt Pru. "Is that you?"

"*Yes,*" he yelled, and decided to run for it.

Too late! There was a heavy *thump, thump, thump* . . .

"Oh my," said Aunt Pru.

"Um, I fell down," said J.J.

"I think you'd better not come inside," said Aunt Pru.

"Then what am I supposed to do?" he cried.

Aunt Pru straightened up. "We'll wash you off," she said. "Go in the back yard."

J.J. groaned. Mom had told him to be extra nice to Aunt Pru. She said that Aunt Pru was really his great-aunt because she was Grandpa Johnson's big sister. But Aunt Pru sure had some weird ideas. Washing him *outside*? Where all the neighbours could see? Was she going to spray him with the hose? It was October. It was *cold*!

J.J. stomped into the back yard. If Aunt Pru really was a great aunt, she'd bake cookies and tell stories. She'd be a nice old lady with white hair.

But Aunt Pru had orange hair. She wore pink powder on her cheeks. She was shaped sort of like a bathtub. She never, *ever* baked cookies. And now she was taking a long time.

"*Grrr!*" said J.J.

At last Aunt Pru appeared with two buckets and some towels. She was huffing and puffing. "Here," she puffed. "This water's warm. Take your shoes and socks off, Jeremy, and stand in this bucket while I wash you."

"Do I have to?" asked J.J.

"Yes," said Aunt Pru.

So he did. He shivered and yelled while Aunt Pru poured the second bucket of water all over him and scrubbed him with a brush.

At last Aunt Pru wrapped him in a blanket. "I'll fix some hot chocolate," she promised. "Now run inside and get changed."

J.J. ran upstairs to his room — and then he remembered. Aunt Pru's clothes were in his closet. Her afghan was spread across his bed.

"Oh barf," J.J. muttered. He went into Jessica's room. When he got a clean shirt out of the closet, Jessica's snowsuit fell on the floor. He looked all over for his *Weirdosaurus* comic and finally found it under Jessica's pink stuffed dog.

A cup of hot chocolate was waiting on the kitchen table. "Thanks," J.J. mumbled.

Aunt Pru gave him a big smile. "Now you look like Jeremy, instead of something the cat dragged in." Her false teeth made little clicking sounds.

J.J. felt like saying something that wasn't very nice. Instead, he sat down and sipped his hot chocolate. It made him feel all warm and cozy inside.

A furry white head with yellow ears and big blue eyes peeked at him from inside one of the cupboards. J.J. couldn't help smiling. He still needed to figure out a name for the kitten.

Chapter 4

The Great Turkey Tackle

Sure enough, Derek was gone over Thanksgiving weekend, and Tanya wasn't home either. The only other kid left in the neighbourhood was Shaun. J.J. read his new *Revenge of Weirdosaurus* comic book at least six times and watched a lot of TV.

After brunch on Thanksgiving morning, Mom sent J.J. outside to play.

He got his skateboard from the garage.

Ka-CHUK, ka-CHUK, ka-CHUK . . .

Wind whooshed past his ears as he rode along the sidewalk. If only he had a dog to run with him. They'd rule the neighbourhood, the invincible J.J. and his faithful dog Spike. Shaun would slink away and hide in the bushes. J.J. and Spike, ridding the neighbourhood of crime.

Ka-CHUK, ka-CHUK . . .

Past Mr. Lim's house.

Ka-CHUK, ka-CHUK . . .

It was good to be out of the house, away from Aunt Pru and her false teeth. He'd even had a dream about those teeth. They had chased him all through the house.

Ka-CHUK, ka-CHUK . . . Life would be great if he could get rid of Aunt Pru.

J.J. stopped and stood there with one foot on his skateboard. Get rid of Aunt Pru? A funny feeling shivered inside him. What would the mastermind J.J. and his loyal sidekick Spike do?

He shook his head and pushed off.

Ka-CHUK, ka-CHUK . . . SCREEEEE!

A black bike blocked his path. Shaun stood waiting for him. "Where's your pit bull, huh?" asked Shaun.

"Um, at home," J.J. said in a hurry. "My dad

won't let me walk him. He's too dangerous."

"Oh sure," said Shaun. "I bet you're lying. Lying fat turkey, all stuffed up. Put you in the oven and watch you sizzle."

J.J. thought about the frozen turkey he'd seen in the fridge. It was a pale chicken colour. The colour of Shaun's face, but he didn't dare say so. "You better watch it, Shaun," he said. "I'll sic Spike on you."

"Who's Spike?" Shaun asked suspiciously.

"My dog," said J.J. He pushed his skateboard through Mrs. Peterson's flower bed to get past Shaun. The plants were frozen, anyhow. He tried not to hurry.

Shaun followed him all the way home. "I don't hear any dog barking," he yelled as J.J. ran to the door.

"Spike can't bark," J.J. said. "He had an operation on his vocal cords. He's more dangerous this way." With luck Mom wouldn't hear.

The house was quiet. "Mom?" J.J. yelled.

No answer.

"*Mom?* Dad?" What had they done, gone off and left him?

No answer. J.J. ran around looking. He peeked into Jessica's room. She was in her crib, having a nap. J.J. tiptoed in to get his *Weirdosaurus Awakes!* comic off the floor.

Strange noises were coming from behind his bedroom door. *Snort-SHEeeeee . . . snort-SHEeeeee . . . snort-snort — SHEeeeee . . .* J.J.'s neck prickled.

What would J.J. and the deadly Spike do? J.J. gulped in a deep breath and opened the door, just a crack.

Aunt Pru lay there sleeping. Her mouth was open. *Snort-SHEeeeee . . .* J.J. shook his head. And now snoring. Some night she'd probably wake him up and scare him to death.

"M-r-r-r-t?"

There was the kitten, cuddled up in a white ball against Aunt Pru's big stomach. That traitor! Didn't he recognize the enemy? "Here, Spike!" J.J. whispered.

The kitten stood up, stretched, and

scampered over to him.

Disgusted, J.J. picked it up. "Where'd Mom go?" he asked.

The kitten didn't answer. It just purred in his ear.

J.J. found the note on the kitchen table.

Dear J.J.,
I've gone to pick up a few things for
Thanksgiving dinner. Aunt Pru is in charge
while I'm gone. I want you to listen to her
and cooperate.
Love, Mom

J.J. had to laugh. Sleeping was a pretty funny way of being in charge. At least he'd already done what Mom told him to. He'd listened to Aunt Pru.

J.J. opened the fridge. He was starving. As he reached for the bread and jam, he saw the turkey. It wasn't frozen any more. J.J. pulled it out so he could look at it.

Gross! The turkey was slimy and cold, and

sort of mushy underneath the skin. Just like Aunt Pru. And Shaun.

J.J. pulled one of the wings and made it flap. There was a big hole in the turkey's middle. You could just about stuff Jessica's little teddy bear in there. It would be an awesome place to hide Aunt Pru's false teeth!

"Meow?" The kitten jumped up on the counter. Its pink nose went crazy sniffing. Before J.J. could stop him, it climbed right on top of the turkey. It looked like it was trying to hug that whole big bird, and couldn't decide where to start eating.

J.J. fell back laughing. He wished he had a camera. Then he thought about where the kitten's paws had been. *"Yuck!"* He grabbed the kitten. The kitten grabbed the turkey and held on with its spiky little claws. "You're going to give us all germs!" he yelled.

In the confusion the turkey fell with a thud and slid across the floor. Upstairs Jessica was yelling "Uuup? Uuup?" Great! She'd wake Aunt Pru!

J.J. grabbed the cold slippery turkey and dumped it in the sink. He ran water over it to rinse off the germs. Then he wrestled it back into the fridge and slammed the door.

"Hello?" Mom was home!

J.J. decided he'd better go play in the basement. As he ran down the stairs, the white kitten scampered by his feet.

"You're no Spike," he muttered. "You're a brat cat. Now we'll all get sick from your germs, and it'll be *your* fault."

Halfway down the stairs he stopped. *Germs!* The ultimate weapon! If Aunt Pru got sick, maybe she'd go away!

Could he get her to go away? The funny feeling shivered through him again. He could make a list of ideas. Germs, plenty of germs. Derek could help him collect them. He could try making weird noises at night. And just maybe, he could hide Aunt Pru's teeth — if he could stand it to touch them.

He had a feeling Mom would ground him till Christmas if she ever found out about this plan.

J.J. went to the kitten's corner. Ever since it started walking across the piano in the middle of the night and digging up the houseplants, Mom said it had to sleep in the basement. The kitten's bed was a laundry basket with an old quilt and some towels. J.J. curled up in a ball and lay in the basket.

This part of the basement was almost like a little room. There was a window, and a light overhead that you could turn on by jumping and pulling a string. There were even some shelves. J.J. lay there and looked out the window. He could see the fence and part of the lilac bush. Overhead Mom was bumping around. Then came the funny little thumpity sounds of Jessica walking.

"M-r-r-r-t?" The kitten climbed on top of him.

J.J. stroked it. "Will you help me solve the Aunt Pru problem?" he asked. But he wouldn't start just yet. He felt so safe and cozy curled up with the kitten in the little room downstairs.

All through Thanksgiving dinner J.J. kept smiling. He couldn't get the picture of the kitten hugging that big turkey out of his mind. But he felt a little sick, too. Had he washed off all the germs?

"Is something wrong, J.J.?" asked Mom.

J.J. pretended to cough. He coughed at Aunt Pru's plate.

"J.J.!" said Dad. "Cover your mouth!"

"Sorry," said J.J.

"Oh, that's all right," said Aunt Pru. "Boys will be boys. It takes me back to when I was little. Come Thanksgiving my papa would go out to the barn and butcher some chickens. I'll never forget the time I looked out the window and saw young Jeremy's grandpa chasing a chicken that had its head cut off."

"What?" J.J. sat up straight, so fast his chair almost tipped over. "Chickens can't run with their heads cut off. They're *dead*."

"Oh yes they can," said Aunt Pru. "Sometimes they'll run around for a bit as if they can't figure out what happened. Then they keel over."

J.J.'s eyes felt as big as the pickle dish. "*Cool! I bet it's *bloody*."

Mom's face was a funny colour.

"Ahem!" said Dad loudly. "Aunt Pru, would you like more turkey?"

"Yes, please," Aunt Pru said. "And a little more—"

But J.J. couldn't wait for her to finish. "Did this turkey run around with its head cut off?"

"Oh no," said Aunt Pru. "These days it's all done in a meat processing plant. The birds are in little cages, and they whack the heads off, *whisht!* with a—"

"Excuse me," Mom interrupted. "I'll get more gravy." She got up. Then Jessica spilled her milk, and J.J. never got to hear the rest of the story. Every time he tried to ask, Dad would interrupt. It made him mad. Until a furry little ball settled in his lap.

"At least you're my friend," J.J. whispered, and handed the kitten a piece of turkey. The kitten's purring got so loud he was afraid Mom would hear. He felt tickly whiskers against his hand, and then sharp teeth grabbed the meat away.

"What did you say, J.J.?" asked Dad.

"Oh, nothing," said J.J. Now the kitten was licking his fingers with its little rough tongue. He tried not to laugh.

"J.J., have you had enough to eat?" Mom asked. "You may be excused if you're done."

"Um . . . " Quickly J.J. dumped the kitten on the floor. He took one last carrot stick. Then he hurried upstairs to plan the Get Rid of Aunt Pru Project. He'd tell Derek all about it tomorrow at school.

Chapter 5

Calling All Germs!

"*B*waaaaaawk - bwaaaaaawk - bwaaaaaawk-bwaaawk!" J.J. was running around in circles, all hunched over and flapping his elbows. Then he fell down on the playground and waved his legs in the air. "I'm dead! I'm dead! They cut off my head!"

Derek was doing the same thing.

"You guys are weird," said Tanya.

"We're chickens," J.J. explained, and sat up. "Chickens can run around with their heads cut off, you know that?"

"They can not."

"Can so," Derek said. "J.J.'s grandpa used to chase them."

"Yeah," said J.J. "Just ask my Aunt Pru."

"Yeah," said Derek, "and we gotta find germs. To give to J.J.'s Auntie Pru-u-u-uneface. Want to help?"

"How come you need germs?" Tanya demanded.

J.J. felt funny about explaining. But he didn't need to worry. Derek was already telling Tanya about their plan. He bent over again and started flapping his wings. "*Bwaaaaaawwwk*-bwaaawk-bwaaawk-bwaaawk . . . "

"That's dumb," Tanya said. "And it's mean, too. What if she *dies*?"

J.J. lay there on the ground. He hadn't thought about that. "She wouldn't die. She'd just get kind of sick and go away."

"Oh yeah? Old people get sick and die, just like that. If you give her germs and she dies, you'll be a *murderer*." Tanya stood there with her jacket flapping in the wind.

"Oh sure," said Derek.

"You'll be murderers. Both of you." Tanya walked away with her chin sticking out and her nose in the air.

Suddenly J.J. didn't feel so good. He lay there looking at the sky.

"She's just scared," said Derek. "She's afraid *she* might get sick. Come on, let's go find — *Look out!*"

There was the sound of running feet. Shaun came at them like a flying monster. J.J. curled up into a ball.

"Turkey meat!" Shaun yelled.

"Owwww!" yelled J.J. as Shaun's foot hit him in the back.

"Ground turkey," said Shaun with a mean laugh. "That's what you are, you turkey brain."

"You better watch it, Shaun," Derek said. "We'll get J.J.'s pit bull, and we'll wait in the bushes right outside your house."

"You're bluffing," Shaun said. "There's no dog at Germy Johnson's house."

J.J. got up fast. "Who says?"

"There is so," Derek said. "J.J. lets me pet him. His name is Fang."

J.J. felt hot and cold at the same time. "*No!*" he cried. "It's Spike, remember? How can you be such a banana brain?"

Shaun was rocking back and forth like a boxer. "Liar, liar, pants on fire. I knew it the whole time. Germy Johnson's too chicken to have a dog."

J.J. was so mad he felt like slugging Shaun.

Shaun spat in the dirt and walked away.

"Why'd you start that pit bull story?" J.J. asked.

"I was only trying to help," said Derek.

J.J. rubbed the kicked place on his back. The story had been kind of fun while it lasted. They'd actually kept Shaun guessing.

Suddenly Derek burst out laughing. "I know where to get germs! Shaun."

"Oh sure," said J.J. "I'll just walk up to Shaun and say, 'Can I touch you? I need some germs for my germ collection.'"

Derek laughed harder. "A germ collection. That's funny. Where would you keep it? You could have a whole germ farm and nobody would even know."

J.J. scratched his head. Where *would* he keep the germs? How did you keep track of something you couldn't even see?

The bell rang. J.J. thought about the problem during silent reading. He thought about it during science. He couldn't keep germs in his pockets. Even if he had a container, how could he be sure the germs would come back out when he needed them? It might be best to touch all kinds of gross things — but *not* Shaun — and never wash his hands. Yeah! That was the answer! And then he'd help Mom set the table for supper.

"Jeremy Johnson."

Uh oh! Mrs. Foley! J.J. blinked. "What?"

Mrs. Foley was at the chalkboard. Kids' names were written down next to names of plants and animals.

"Are you with us, Jeremy? Something gave

me the distinct impression that you were out in space."

J.J. felt his neck getting hot. "Um—"

"I'll ask you one more time, Jeremy. What form of life would you like to study for your science report?"

"Um—" J.J.'s neck got hotter. Everybody was staring at him. One of the girls giggled. "Um—" And then he knew. It was perfect! "Germs!" he cried.

"That's fine, Jeremy. Next time please don't shout." Beside his name Mrs. Foley put *germs* in neat yellow writing.

"*Germy Johnson!*" Kyle whispered.

J.J. glared at him. But then he realized that he *wanted* to be germy — just as long as *he* didn't get sick!

J.J. had a great time the rest of that afternoon. He crawled around on the floor after school, when nobody was looking. He dug in the dirt. On his way home he petted lots of dogs and cats. He looked in people's garbage and found a slightly cracked hockey stick and several pop cans, which he dumped in the recycling bin. He even offered to change Jessica's diaper.

By supper time his hands were a peculiar greyish colour. "I'll set the table, Mom," he said.

Mom looked surprised. "That would be nice, J.J. Make sure you wash your hands first."

Wash his hands? After going to all that trouble? J.J. ran to the bathroom and turned on the water. Then he ran back downstairs and got some plates. He put them on the table, and rubbed his hand all over Aunt Pru's plate.

The kitten jumped from somewhere and began climbing his jogging pants. J.J. bent over to pet it. It bothered him that the kitten still didn't have a name.

"J.J.!" Mom caught his wrist. "You just washed! Now put that cat down and go scrub your hands again."

"Um, sorry," said J.J. Upstairs he went, with the kitten scampering along by his feet. He scrubbed everything this time except one thumb. Grey suds ran down the drain. When he dried his hands, he left grey smudges on the towel. The kitten jumped at the dangling towel. J.J. hung it up and hurried downstairs. Mom was wiping all the plates.

She looked at his hands. "Much better."

J.J. got out the knives and forks and spoons. When he set Aunt Pru's place, he rubbed his dirty thumb on her fork.

Mom came out just then with a big platter of leftover turkey. "What are you doing, J.J.?" she asked.

"Um, wiping some dirt off this fork," he said. "Something was stuck on it."

"Let's see." Mom reached for the fork. "I don't see anything. But better put it in the sink. We don't want to be eating with dirty silverware." And then she saw J.J.'s thumb. "J.J.," she said, "didn't I tell you — *twice* — to wash your hands?"

"I guess I forgot my thumb," J.J. mumbled.

Mom sighed and shook her head.

J.J. sighed too. Maybe the germ plan wouldn't be as simple as he'd thought!

Chapter 6

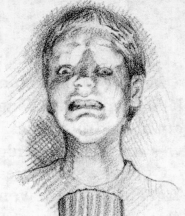

Dreams and Scary Noises

So far the germs hadn't worked. Aunt Pru was as healthy as ever. And Tanya was going around school saying that J.J. was a jerk for trying to get rid of his old aunt.

But J.J. wasn't about to give up on the Get Rid of Aunt Pru Project. Sharing a room with Jessica was worse than he'd expected. She ripped his comic books. She kept putting his Lego pieces in her mouth until Mom put the box up high in the closet. Now he couldn't reach it either. And Jessica went to bed at 7:00. After that, J.J. wasn't allowed in except to sleep.

Mom kept telling him to be patient. J.J. figured he'd been patient long enough. It was time he got his bedroom back. The next thing on his list was scary noises at night.

Quiet as a spy, J.J. reached for his alarm clock. Tonight Aunt Pru would get the surprise of her life. Carefully he set the alarm for 2:30 in the morning.

When the alarm went, he'd sneak out in the hall with his secret weapons. The empty ravioli can and the big spoon made a cool clattering sound. The empty paper towel roll was great for groaning into. And then, with his flashlight, he'd make the scary faces that he'd learned from Derek.

J.J. lay there for a long time. Finally he heard the *thump-squeak*, *thump-squeak* of Aunt Pru coming upstairs. She sounded as slow and big as a brontosaurus. After a while J.J. heard his bed creak. What if Aunt Pru broke it?

J.J. pretended to snore, but it didn't sound right. Soon he heard the real thing coming from his bedroom. And in her crib Jessica was making tiny baby snores.

J.J. thought about the false teeth. Every night Aunt Pru left them soaking in a special container. In his mind, the teeth seemed to grin at him. J.J. shivered.

Mom and Dad came upstairs. "I wouldn't worry about it," Dad was saying. "Wouldn't *you* be mad if you were a kid and had to give up your bedroom?"

They were talking about him! J.J. lay still and listened.

" . . . long time." Mom was hard to hear. " . . . toys . . . keep . . . "

J.J. listened harder but now it was quiet. His eyes started feeling heavy. Then they blinked open again.

" . . . take it in stride," Dad was saying.

" . . . doesn't make it any easier for J.J.," Mom replied.

They didn't say anything after that. J.J. lay there in the dark. On the other side of the wall, the steady *snort-SHEeeeee* continued. At last he fell asleep.

He dreamed he was in his bedroom, building a Lego fort. Aunt Pru's false teeth sat on his bed. They were huge. And for some reason, his *Weirdosaurus* comic was covered with germs. The germs were so big he could see them.

Suddenly the teeth clicked and flashed. They began to grow. The germs started crawling toward him.

In the dream J.J. tried to run away. But he couldn't.

"*No!*" he screamed. Now the germs were crawling all over him. Aunt Pru's teeth were as big as Dad's desk. Open — shut — open — shut. Click, click, click. They were coming for him! "*Aaaauughhhhh!*"

J.J. woke up. His heart was thumping and he was covered with sweat. The dream seemed so real he wished he could crawl in bed with Mom and Dad where it was safe.

"Day-day," said Jessica in a sleepy voice.

What on earth was she talking about? It wasn't day. It was night, and kind of scary. J.J. almost got up to turn on the light.

Then he heard footsteps. The door slowly opened. A dark shape appeared in the doorway. J.J. nearly yelled again. But it was just Aunt Pru.

"Did you have a bad dream, Jeremy?" Aunt Pru asked. She didn't have her teeth in. J.J. could tell by the way she talked.

"Yeah," he said.

Aunt Pru sat down on the cot beside him. "Want to talk about it? You scared me half to death when you cried out!"

Why didn't Mom come? He couldn't tell Aunt Pru that he'd had a scary dream about her teeth! He shivered.

Aunt Pru noticed. "Let's go down to the kitchen," she said. "I'll fix you some hot chocolate."

A few minutes later J.J. was sitting at the table drinking hot chocolate. There was a marshmallow floating in it. J.J. wondered how many germs were on that marshmallow. He shuddered. But the hot chocolate was great. Slowly the shivery feeling went away.

"Feeling better now, J.J.?" asked Aunt Pru.

J.J. nodded. He bit into the marshmallow. "I dreamed about giant germs," he said. "They were crawling all over me and—" He stopped. He just couldn't tell the part about the teeth.

By the time the hot chocolate was done J.J. was sleepy again.

"Day-day," said Jessica when he got back to bed.

"It's night," said J.J. "Can't you tell? It's dark."

Jessica laughed. "Day-day," she said. "Day-day, Day-day!"

How could he go back to sleep if she kept talking? J.J. thought about going down to the basement to sleep with the kitten. Except it was dark down there. And the furnace made growly noises.

Soon the familiar *snort-SHEeeeee* was coming from his bedroom. Aunt Pru was snoring again. At least he'd scared her!

Suddenly there was a loud ringing under the cot.

The alarm clock! J.J. turned it off in a hurry.

Jessica laughed. "Day-day!" she said. Now she was standing up in her crib, bouncing.

All of a sudden J.J. understood. "Jessica! You said my name!"

It made him feel pretty good. He gave Jessica a hug. Then he crawled back in bed. After all, 2:30 in the morning was a silly time to be awake.

Chapter 7

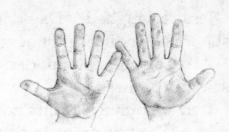

A Bad Day

"J.J.!" snapped Mom. "I've told you three times. *Eat* your food, don't play with it. And keep that cat off the table."

Brother! It was breakfast time, and Mom was acting like a witch! She knew he hated scrambled eggs, so why was she making him eat them? Jessica was on the kitchen floor with a bowl of Cheerios. Mom didn't care if *she* played with her food. *She* didn't have to eat yucky eggs.

The kitten stuck its cold wet nose into J.J.'s

face. "At least *you're* not mean," J.J. told the kitten. It purred.

"*J.J.!*" said Mom. "I'll have a word with you upstairs."

"It's just that Aunt Pruneface has to wreck everything," J.J. said when Mom was finished. "You won't even let Derek come over."

"I'm sorry," said Mom. "I just haven't had time to . . . " She shook her head. "That's no excuse for you to forget your manners, though."

J.J. was surprised that Mom didn't yell at him for calling names. He almost felt bad. Aunt Pru wasn't a pruneface, not really. She didn't even get grouchy.

"When can I have my room back?" he asked. It seemed like forever since he'd slept in his own bed.

Mom sighed. "I don't know, J.J. Aunt Pru is waiting for a condo in Maple Village. It might be a long time."

"Oh, barf," said J.J. But he wasn't as mad as he wanted to be. Aunt Pru couldn't go back to her old house in Saskatoon. It had been torn down for a highway. Even the trees were gone.

He looked at his hands. Right now they'd be full of kitten germs. He had a feeling all those germs wouldn't make any difference. When he'd looked up germs for his report, the encyclopedia said that most kinds of germs didn't make people sick.

He'd have to come up with another plan.

"Can you come over after school?" J.J. whispered across the aisle to Derek. Mrs. Foley was marking papers.

Derek grinned. "You mean 'Project Germ' actually worked?"

"I hear two boys talking," said Mrs. Foley. She did not look up.

J.J. shook his head. His new plan was to invite lots of friends over every day and keep the house noisy. Maybe that would make Aunt Pru leave. He turned his paper over and wrote SHE'S STILL HERE on the other side. Tanya saw it too.

Derek looked confused. "Then how come—"

"Derek Scott," said Mrs. Foley. "If I hear one more peep out of you, you can keep me company after school." She started walking around the room.

J.J. began colouring with his orange marker. The class was making covers for their science reports, but his didn't look like much. Oh well. Germs didn't look like much, either. Even the microscope pictures weren't anything to get excited about.

Mrs. Foley stopped by his desk. "And what, Jeremy, is *that*?" she asked.

"Germs," J.J. said in a hurry. His face got hot. He drew a green blob with squiggly legs. "Is that better?"

"That's fine, Jeremy." Mrs. Foley walked away.

J.J. looked at his drawing. He had a feeling Mrs. Foley didn't like it. He crumpled the paper and started over.

At last the bell rang. J.J. hurried outside. But Derek was taking a long time. Had Mrs. Foley kept him in?

Tanya walked up. "I hope your aunt *doesn't* get sick," she said. "Not ever."

"Aunt Pru's not so bad, I guess," J.J. mumbled.

Right away Tanya was friendlier. "What did you name your kitten?" she asked.

J.J. looked at the ground. "He hasn't got a name yet." He felt funny about that. Somehow finding a name hadn't seemed as important as getting rid of Aunt Pru.

"Can I come see it?" said Tanya. "Maybe I can think of something."

J.J. doubted it. Then Derek came charging out the door. "Gimme five!" he yelled, and held out his hand.

J.J. slapped it. "What took you so long?"

Derek fell back laughing. "Now you've got some *super* germs! Mr. Schmidt's class was cleaning out the rat cage. I helped."

"*GROSS!*" J.J. yelled. He wiped his hands on his jeans.

Shaun was watching. "What's bugging you, Germy Johnson?"

J.J.'s fists clenched. Then he thought of something. "Nothing you'd be interested in," he said. "Just another specimen."

"Yeah," said Derek. "J.J.'s collecting all kinds of deadly germs. We're saving them just for you, Shaun."

Shaun gave them a funny look and went to bug somebody else.

J.J. and Derek laughed all the way to Cameron Street. Even Tanya couldn't seem to stop laughing.

Mom's car was gone.

J.J. grinned. Perfect!

Chapter 8

Those Teeth!

Aunt Pru met them at the door, big as a bathtub. "My, J.J.," she said. "You've brought some friends. How nice."

Derek stared at Aunt Pru.

J.J. shivered. He hoped Derek wouldn't ask about her teeth.

"Where's your kitten?" asked Tanya.

The kitten was halfway up the drapes. Jessica laughed and pointed. "Gee!" she cried. "Gee!"

Uh oh, J.J. thought. Mom would be mad — if she were home to see.

"I'll go fix you kids some sandwiches," said Aunt Pru.

Tanya got the kitten down. "Hi," she said. "You're cute." She petted it. "What's your name? Snowflake? Wiggles?"

"Those are dumb names." J.J. took the kitten from Tanya and rolled around on the floor with it.

"My," huffed Aunt Pru as she walked in with a plate full of sandwiches. "You must be feeling good, young fella."

Jessica walked over on her wobbly little legs and tried to catch the kitten. Suddenly the kitten's sharp claws poked into J.J.'s stomach. "Owwww!" yelled J.J. "You brat cat!"

"He's just a young scallywag," said Aunt Pru. "Hasn't learned his manners yet."

Derek took a huge bite of peanut butter sandwich. "Is it true chickens can run around with their heads cut off?" he said through a mouthful of peanut butter. He swallowed. "Did you ever see it?"

"Oh my, yes," said Aunt Pru. She started

telling her Thanksgiving story all over again. Tanya's eyes got big.

"Told you," said J.J.

When Aunt Pru finished, Derek asked to see her teeth.

"Good heavens!" said Aunt Pru. "Haven't you ever seen false teeth?" She reached in her mouth. Out came her top teeth, sitting in a neat row. Out came her bottom teeth.

"*Cool!*" said Derek.

J.J. ran upstairs. Just the sight of those teeth gave him the shivers. He grabbed his remote control Z-28 and ran back downstairs. He drove his car in circles while Aunt Pru talked about her teeth.

There was a white blur, and the kitten tackled the car. J.J. laughed and set it on turbo charge. *Vroooom!* The Z-28 roared across the room. It crashed into a lamp pole . . .

Mom walked in with three big bags of groceries just as the lamp crashed down on the TV.

"Oh my," said Aunt Pru. She put her teeth back in and hurried over to pick up the lamp.

Nothing was broken.

"Uh oh." J.J. wished he could disappear.

"What's going on in here?" asked Mom.

She glared at J.J. She glared at Derek and Tanya. Then she set the groceries down.

Derek headed for the door.

"I have to go too," Tanya said, and followed Derek.

The kitten sniffed at one of the bags. Mom didn't notice. She didn't even notice when Jessica started pulling things out of another bag. The only thing she seemed interested in was J.J., and she looked so mad J.J. was afraid she'd turn him into a frog. Or a turkey.

"I've had it!" Mom said. "What's the matter with you? Every time you're out of my sight, something happens. You come home covered with mud. The Thanksgiving turkey's wing gets mysteriously broken. Mrs. Peterson complains that you were in her flower bed. You set your alarm for peculiar hours. Your manners have been *terrible*. And now this!"

"But—" J.J. protested.

"I'm sure it was an accident," said Aunt Pru.

Mom didn't seem to care. "Your father and I are going out tonight," she said, looking straight at J.J. "Aunt Pru is babysitting. You are to have *no* friends over. You are *not* to go outside. I don't want any more trouble. Do you understand? I want you in bed by seven-thirty."

J.J. groaned in dismay. Could things get any worse?

Chapter 9

A Special Place

Aunt Pru fixed supper that night. She made J.J.'s favourite, macaroni with tons of cheese and little hot dog wheels. But J.J. wasn't hungry.

Why was Mom being so mean? It was even worse than having Aunt Pru around! Maybe he could run away and live at Derek's house.

J.J. left the table. He'd only eaten a few bites. His stomach felt like somebody was walking on it with big boots.

He went down to the basement and turned on the light. The kitten's basket was empty. J.J. flopped into it and curled up in a little ball.

"M-r-r-t?" The kitten came from somewhere and started walking on him.

J.J. didn't have the energy to pet it.

"Jeremy? J.J.?" Aunt Pru was calling. When he didn't answer, she kept right on calling.

"WHAT?" he yelled at last.

THUMP-creeak, THUMP-creeak went the basement steps. J.J. stayed curled up in the laundry basket. Maybe Aunt Pru wouldn't find him.

But she did. "Oh, *there* you are," she said.

Aunt Pru sat down on an old chair left over from the kitchen. The chair creaked. "I'm sure your mama didn't mean to be sharp with you, J.J.," she said after a minute. "It's hard on her, having an old lady like me around."

Hard on Mom? So what? Mom still had her bedroom. J.J. didn't say anything. He coughed instead, and it wasn't completely on purpose. His throat was sore.

Aunt Pru patted his shoulder. "I know it's hard on you, young fella. I feel bad about taking your room."

To his horror, J.J. began to cry. He couldn't

seem to stop. So he climbed into Aunt Pru's lap. She didn't smell so much like medicine any more. She smelled like . . . Aunt Pru.

"It's all right," Aunt Pru said over and over again. She hugged him and patted his shoulder, and her teeth made little clicking sounds. "I'm sure your mama must feel just awful about what she said."

"She-she does not!" J.J. got the hiccups. He hiccupped and cried at the same time. At last it stopped.

The kitten jumped into J.J.'s lap, purring like a motor. J.J. put his nose by the kitten's cold little nose, and felt its prickly whiskers.

"Have you named your kitten yet?" asked Aunt Pru.

"No," J.J. mumbled. Then he thought of something. He sat up straighter. "You called him something this afternoon. A young scorly — a skilly-wig — no, what was it?"

"I remember," said Aunt Pru. "I said he was a young scallywag who hadn't learned his manners."

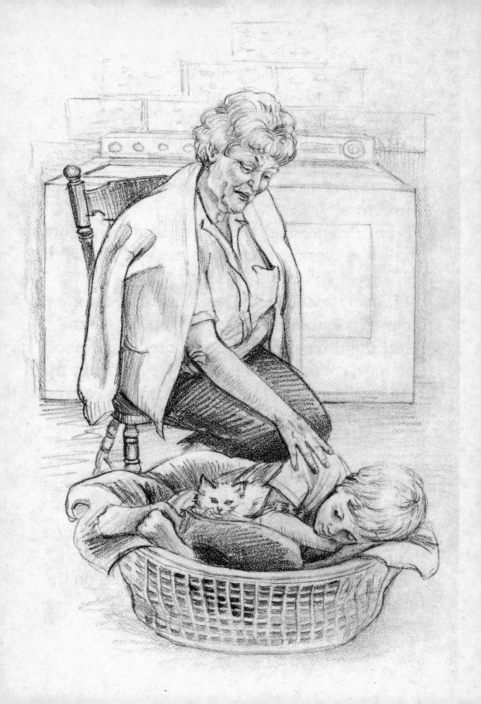

"Yeah!" In his excitement, J.J. tipped right out of Aunt Pru's lap into the basket. "Scallywag! That's what I'll call him." Now that he had a name for the kitten, he felt better.

But that didn't mean things would be better with Mom.

Aunt Pru seemed to read J.J.'s mind. "Now don't you worry about your mama," she said. "She loves you a whole bunch."

J.J. drew a Z-28 with laser beam headlights. He put it on the dining room table for Mom.

But there was no way he wanted to sleep on that hard cot again. Not even if Jessica woke up in the night and said his name. After his bath he went back down to the basement and plugged in a night light. Then he curled up in the laundry basket and fell asleep.

Much later he heard footsteps on the basement stairs. It sounded like Mom.

J.J. lay there and pretended to be asleep. Even though his throat tickled and scratched.

Even when Mom gave him a nice kiss on the forehead.

Chapter 10

Aunt Pru, I Love You

J.J. felt awful the next morning. His throat was sore. He had a cough. His head ached. And he was all stiff from sleeping in the laundry basket.

He got up. The basement stairs felt unusually steep. There seemed to be an awful lot of steps.

Mom met him in the hallway. "Thank you for the beautiful picture, J.J.," she said, and gave him a hug. "That's a very fancy car. I've put it on the fridge so we can all see it. And J.J., I'm sorry about yesterday. I was having a bad day. I shouldn't have taken it out on you."

J.J. coughed.

"Oh my goodness," said Mom. "Are you sick again, J.J.?"

J.J. nodded. His legs felt like applesauce. What he really wanted to do was crawl in bed — but now it was Aunt Pru's bed.

"Come," said Mom. "You can lie down on the couch. After breakfast I'll put some clean sheets on Dad's and my bed, and you can rest there."

J.J. nodded. The germ idea must have backfired!

"Feeling poorly, J.J.?" Aunt Pru asked as he went by. As usual, she was in the rocking chair, wearing her bathrobe and reading the paper.

J.J. lay down. The couch felt wonderful.

Dad came in with a coffee mug in his hand. "Not feeling so great, J.J.?"

J.J. shook his head.

Dad patted him on the head. "At least you've found yourself a bedroom. Not such a bad idea, actually — as long as you have a decent bed to sleep in."

J.J. sat up. A bedroom? In the basement? It was almost a scary idea. But he'd already slept there one night, and the furnace hadn't bothered him. Or the dark, either. Besides, he'd had company. All night Scallywag had been there, a warm furry lump cuddled against him.

"Think about it," said Dad. "We can fix it up for you." And then he was off to the TV station where he worked.

J.J. wasn't hungry, but Mom brought him some orange juice anyway. It hurt his throat.

Jessica climbed up with him. "Day-day!" she cried. She looked very proud at being able to say his name. J.J. gave her a weak smile.

"Oh no you don't, young miss!" Aunt Pru scooped Jessica off. "Can't have you bothering your big brother. Besides, we don't want you getting sick."

Suddenly Mom was there too. She reached for Jessica and turned to Aunt Pru. "You'd better not get too close either, Aunt Pru. We don't want you getting sick."

J.J. looked at his feet. He felt very peculiar. After all his efforts, he suddenly knew that he didn't want Aunt Pru to get sick either.

Aunt Pru just laughed. "Oh, don't worry about me. I'm so old and tough those germs have given up. Why, I haven't been sick in ten years!"

J.J. fell asleep. Arguing voices awakened him later.

" . . . pack my bags. I'm nothing but a nuisance. Just look at the young fella. He's sick, and doesn't even have a proper bed."

"No, Aunt Pru," Mom said. "We'll work things out."

"No," said Aunt Pru. "I had no business imposing on you. Don't worry about me. I'll take a hotel room until—"

"We'll work things out," Mom said again.

Aunt Pru had a funny look on her face. "It's been so nice staying with your family. But I'm an old lady. I've been nothing but a pest to you all. I'll start packing my bags."

Was Aunt Pru going? J.J. sat up fast, even though it made his head feel like it would explode. "No!" he cried. "Don't go, Aunt Pru!" He ran into the kitchen and hugged her hard, then looked up into her wrinkled old face. "Please?"

And then he said something he'd never, ever expected to say. "I love you, Aunt Pru."

"Oh well, now." Aunt Pru's voice sounded all crackly. She hugged him back. J.J. could hear her breathing. "I love you too, young fella." Her teeth clicked, but for some reason it didn't bother J.J. any more. The next time he looked up, big tears were rolling down Aunt Pru's cheeks.

"See?" said Mom with a smile. "The kids want you to stay. Your place is with us, Aunt Pru. For as long as you want."

"Yeah," said J.J. He coughed, but he made sure he coughed *away* from Aunt Pru. "You can have my bedroom as long as you want, too."

After all, Dad had said they could fix up the basement. That would be cool. He was old enough to sleep downstairs by himself — and anyhow, he'd have Scallywag for company.

Aunt Pru gave J.J. another hug. "I'll think about it," she promised. "We'll give it a few more days."

"Good." J.J. stood there with his head leaning

against Aunt Pru. But something was climbing the legs of his pajamas. He looked down. "You little brat cat!"

Aunt Pru held Scallywag in front of her face and looked at him sternly. "Now you listen to me, Scallywag. This young fella is my favourite grand-nephew, and I won't have you pestering him. Do you promise to be good?"

J.J. had to laugh. Scallywag's two blue eyes were wide and staring, full of mischief. As J.J. watched, a little white paw reached out and batted at Aunt Pru's orange hair.

He shook his finger at the kitten. "Now listen to me," he said. "Aunt Pru is my very favourite great-aunt. She's *great*. And you better not bug her either!"

It was true. Aunt Pru was great. Having her around was like having an extra grandma.

It seemed like a long time since J.J. had thought about having a dog. With Aunt Pru and Scallywag around to liven things up, who needed a dog?

**Other books in the
Shooting Star series:**